Kazuo Iwamura

HOORAY for FALL!

NorthSouth
New York / London

Deep in the woods, summer was over.
Mick, Mack, and Molly were going with
Papa to collect nuts.

When they came home, their baskets were full.
"Look, Mama!" said Mick. "We found so many nuts!"
Mama had been busy too.
"What are you knitting?" asked Mack.
"It's a secret," said Mama. "You'll have to wait and
see when I have finished."

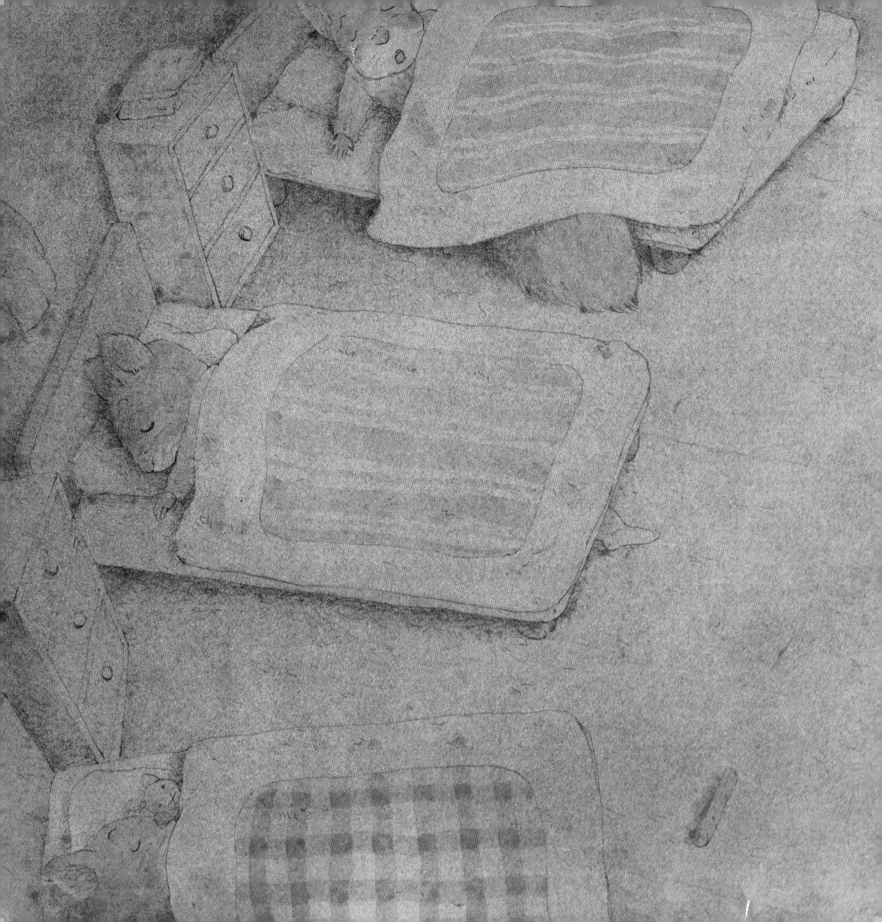

That night, the little squirrels were tired out.
They fell asleep as soon as they went to bed.
    "It's beginning to get cold already," said Papa.
    "Winter is coming," said Mama. "I must
hurry." And she knitted late into the night.

The next morning, Mama called her children.

"I finished them last night," she said. "Now try on these sweaters."

"What great red sweaters!" said Mick.

"Don't we look nice in the same sweaters," said Molly.

"I'm stuck, " Mack squeaked, and everyone laughed.

When they all had on their sweaters, they went outside into the woods.

"Hello, birds!" said Mick. "Look at our handsome sweaters!"

"Aren't they beautiful!" said Molly. "They match!"

"Our mama knitted them for us," said Mack.

"Soon it will be cold, but you will be really warm
this winter," said the mama bird.

"We are flying south to a warm place," chirped
the bird children. "See you next year!"

"Look at the mushrooms!" shouted Mick.

"They have red sweaters, just like us!" said Molly.

"And they are just like our family too," said Mack.

"A mama and a papa and three children."

"I found some red berries!" cried Mack. "*Really* red berries."

"The last time we were here, they were green, weren't they?" asked Mick.

"Winter is coming, so they changed their clothes, just like us," said Molly.

"They are as red as our sweaters!" shouted Mack.

"Even the leaves are red!" said Molly.

"Does everything change color because cold winter is coming?" said Mick.

"That's it!" said Mack. "Everything turns red, just like us in our sweaters!"

A little farther on, a bear was eating red persimmons.

"How can you eat so many?" asked Molly. "Don't you get a tummyache?" She was worried.

"Oh, no," said the bear. "I need to eat a lot. Bears sleep during the winter, so I have to eat plenty now."

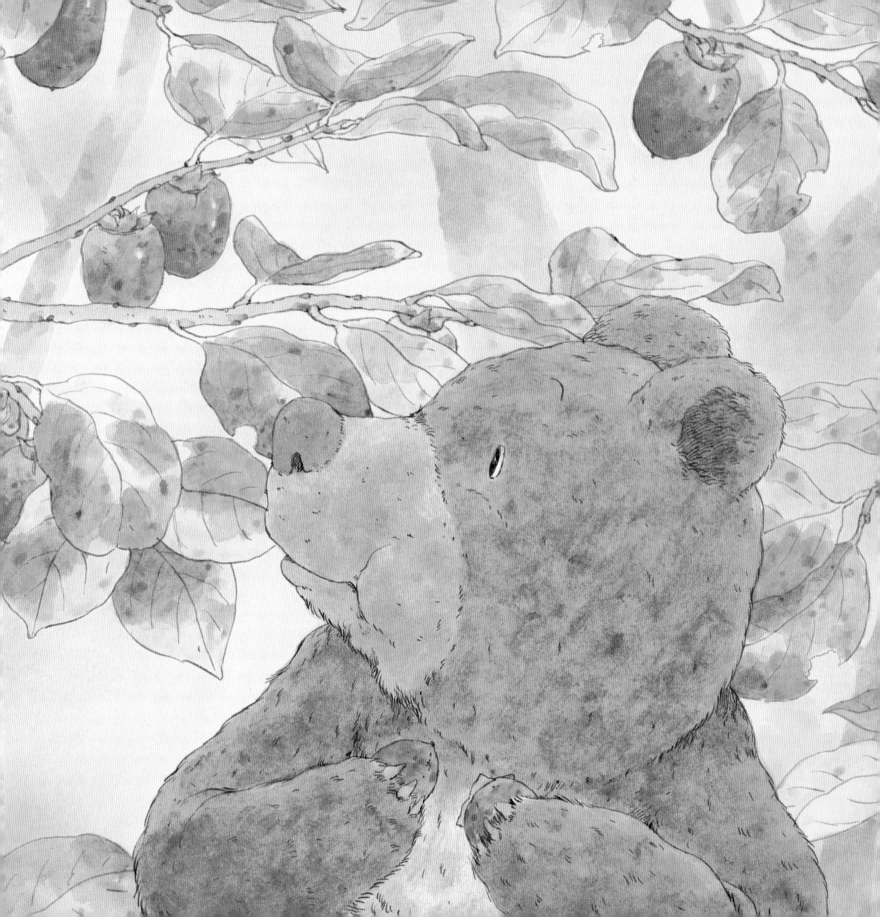

"Oh, dear!" cried Molly. "Look over there!"

"The sky is on fire!" Mack shouted.

And sure enough, up in the sky was a great red glow.

"Let's climb up to the treetop and see what it is," said Mick.

That night, the little squirrels couldn't wait to tell Mama and Papa about their day.

"The berries are red!" said Mack. "Just like our sweaters."

"The leaves are red!" said Molly. "Just like our sweaters."

"Even the sky is red!" said Mick. "Just like our sweaters."

"That's because winter is coming," said Mama.

"That's because it's fall," said Papa.

"Hooray for fall!" said Mick and Mack and Molly.

Late that night, after the children had gone to bed, Papa and Mama sat by the stove.

"What are you knitting now?" Papa asked Mama.

"Something for you, my dear," said Mama. "A red scarf!"

And all winter long, no matter how cold it got, the squirrel family kept warm in their red sweaters and scarf.

Copyright © 1984 by Kazuo Iwamura.
English translation copyright © 2009 by North-South Books Inc., New York 10001.
All rights reserved.
No part of this book may be reproduced or utilized in any form or by any means, electronic or mechanical,
including photo-copying, recording, or any information storage and retrieval system,
without permission in writing from the publisher.
First published in Japan in 1984 by Shiko-Sha Co., Ltd., Tokyo,
under the title *Makkana Seetaa*.
Published in the United States, Great Britain, Canada, Australia, and New Zealand in 2009 by North-South Books Inc.,
an imprint of NordSüd Verlag AG, CH-8005 Zürich, Switzerland.
Distributed in the United States by North-South Books Inc., New York 10001.
Library of Congress Cataloging-in-Publication Data is available.
Printed in China by Toppan Leefung Packaging & Printing (Dongguan) Co., Ltd., Dongguan, P.R.C., May 2010.
ISBN: 978-0-7358-2252-8 (trade edition).
10 9 8 7 6 5 4 3 2

www.northsouth.com